Illustrated by:
BARBARA BONGINI

written by:
CASEY WIEGAND

ANNEMARIE'S
Make-Believe

Edited by Lindsay Schlegel
Layout by Lucy Featherstone
Illustrations © Good & True Media
ISBN: 978-1-955492-76-8
Kindle ISBN: 978-1-955492-94-2
EPUB ISBN: 978-1-955492-95-9
Audiobook (Retail): 978-1-955492-96-6
Audiobook (Library): 978-1-955492-97-3

Printed in India
Published in the United States by
Good & True Media
PO Box 269
Gastonia, NC 28053
www.GoodandTrueMedia.com

*To my family,*
*My husband Chris and our four children:*
*Aiden, Ainsleigh, Apple & Adelaide.....*
*you all are my heart, my world, my everything!*
*Continue to be a light to the world, be the sunshine!*

There once lived a young girl named AnneMarie.
She was amazing, for she had unlocked a very powerful imagination.

Some days, she would imagine the clouds hopping across
the sky like bunnies, and other days she would imagine
sunflowers shining at her like the sun.

One beautiful day in Maple Springs,
a new family moved in next door.
AnneMarie saw a young girl about her age
get out of the truck and smile at her.
Instead of saying "Hi," AnneMarie's face turned beet red
as she ran inside her playhouse, The Tea Cottage.

She thought about going over to say, "Hi,"
but fear swelled in her stomach as a
large lion stepped down from
the back of the moving truck!

The lion growled and began pacing back
and forth in front of the house as if
guarding one of its cubs.

"I know, I know... how embarrassing...." AnneMarie said as she began making some tea. Of course, there was no tea in it, but a girl like AnneMarie could always pretend.

"You don't have to look at me like that, Archie." She poured tea from her teapot. "And you, Rosie, you know not everyone can be as talkative as you all the time."

AnneMarie found that the best conversations always happened over tea. As AnneMarie poured the warm drink, Rosie shook her head, and a huge smile spread over her lips.

"Mmmmmm, I love the smell of your tea, AnneMarie," Rosie said, now fully animated and alive thanks to AnneMarie's imagination.

Next, AnneMarie filled Archie's cup up.

As AnneMarie took a seat, she couldn't help but frown.

"AnneMarie, what is wrong? You love people more than
anyone I know. Did something happen at
school today, my dear?"

She shifted in her seat, knowing the question was coming.

"Someone passed me a mean note in class today.
It called me names, and it really hurt my feelings...."

Beautiful
beautiful
Beautiful
YOU
ARE A
TREASURE
Shine
your
LiGHT
Spread
the
SUNSHINE

"Words can hurt. I am so sorry that happened to you ...but you know words can heal also."

"I am glad that you only pass kind notes! Like these affirmations, you have all over the wall here! You see how much words can mean," Rosie explained.

"I want to say hi to my new neighbor! But what if she doesn't like me? And what about that lion?" AnneMarie pleaded.

"You can conquer a lion, my dear. You just have to find the right words of inspiration." Archie explained.

"And you know what that means...."

"It's time for another trip to the Make-Believe?"
AnneMarie asked, and Archie nodded. Rosie, however, jumped for joy.

"Yay yay yay!!! I LOVE the Make-Believe!"

"I suppose you are right. We need to find some more words!"
AnneMarie exclaimed.

"The right words, my dear... they live deep inside of you, now let's go find them."

And with that, they all put their hands on the tea pot, and it started glowing!

"This place is beautiful! This is your imagination, Anne-Marie? Amazing!" Rosie marveled at the sight.

"Let's go find some words!" AnneMarie replied, excited to be back in her Make-Believe.

"The right words, my dear... the right words," Archie replied.

"Why are words so important?" AnneMarie asked.

"They touch the heart, either for good or for bad,"
Rosie replied. "Someone made you feel bad today, I know. But
that doesn't mean that you shouldn't keep spreading the
sunshine that you are."

"She's right, you know...." Archie added.

You are a

creation

of

"Look! There are some words there!... You are a creation of..."
Rosie pointed to the sky.

"What do you think that means, AnneMarie?" Archie asked.
She considered it for a minute and replied.

"I think it means that God created me thoughtfully. I am special and unique. God created me with a purpose."

"That's right... your purpose matters!" Archie replied.

"But it says 'You are a creation of...'
of what?" she asked.

"Hmmm I'm not sure..." Rosie muttered.

"I guess that is one of the best questions someone
could ask themselves." Archie replied.

"There it is... your answer."
Rosie exclaimed, pointing towards three
treasure chests.

"What am I a creation of?" AnneMarie asked,
as she moved to open the chests.

But before she could, a fierce lion jumped out of the trees.
It was the lion from next door!

"Oh no! Oh no! Oh noooo!"
Rosie wailed, folding her ears over her eyes.

"No!" AnneMarie stepped forward.
"It's okay, Rosie. We're in my Make-Believe...
I'm in control here," she explained.

"I realize that I'm a creation of God.
And this lion... well, this lion is my creation, he represents my fears. And this lion is fear. So I have made myself afraid when I shouldn't be."

AnneMarie fearlessly walked up to the lion
and began petting it.

It stopped growling and laid down for her, purring like a kitten.
"What courage you have, my dear," Archie praised.

Rosie, who was still terrified, poked an eye from behind her paws.
She couldn't believe the lion laid down for AnneMarie.

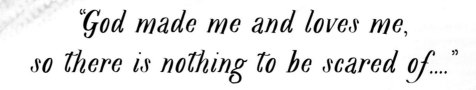

"God made me and loves me,
so there is nothing to be scared of...."

She stepped up from the lion and walked to the chests.

"Ohhh what's in the chests!?"
Rosie couldn't contain herself any longer.

"You're a creation of Love, Truth and Beauty...."

"Yes, you are AnneMarie." Rosie teared up with a smile.

"I think you have found the right words, my dear."
Archie smiled as well.

"I am a creation of love, truth and beauty..."
At the sound of the words, a feeling of joy filled her.
She felt like a shining sun, ready to light up the world.

When AnneMarie returned to the real world,
she checked the window again and looked for
the lion next door.

But there was no lion anymore, it was just a harmless house cat all along. AnneMarie knew that her imagination had gotten away from her again. Fear was the lion, and it was quieted with the truth.

Saying hello to the new neighbour didn't have to be scary at all, and in fact, it looked like the girl next door would love a new friend.

A smile came to AnneMarie's lips, as she finally knew what to do. She looked at her wall of inspiration for the perfect words and snatched them off the wall.

AnneMarie made a new friend that day. And she never would have worked up the courage if she didn't find the inspiration inside of her.

She now knew that she was a creation of love, truth and beauty, and she was excited to share it with others.

## *About the Author*

Casey Wiegand lives in Dallas, Texas with her family. She is a mama to four children, wife, artist, creator, and dreamer. She has been sharing her life online for years and has a passion for families, for creativity, and for encouraging others to share their gifts. Somes of Casey's favourite things are sunshine, the color pink, her grandma's old quilts, staying in her pj's by a cozy fire, pink cupcakes and encouraging others to shine their light.

Casey's personal mission is to spread kindness wherever she goes, which is what inspired her book, *AnneMarie's Make-Believe*, she hopes that her book will remind everyone that they have the power to spread *kindness* and *love* wherever they go and whomever they meet. Spread your sunshine!

GOOD & TRUE

M E D I A

## About the Publisher

Good & True Media aims to educate the imagination of children through fun, thought-provoking stories built on a strong moral foundation. We are dedicated to deepening the mind, moving the heart and strengthening the soul of children. We foster wonder in children so that they can pursue a virtuous life. By publishing new value-based stories with a strong moral message and by republishing classic works in a way that makes the stories of old new and accessible to a modern audience, we are able to be the positive influence parents need when entrusting their children to media.

Good & True is a proudly Christian company that seeks to shape the future of children's literature. Launched in 2021, we are only beginning our journey, but we pledge to remain steadfast in our core purpose—to help children grow in virtue.

For exclusive content, promotions, and sneak peeks of our forthcoming titles, subscribe to our newsletter.

SCAN ME